Miss Wire and the Three Kind Mice

IAN WHYBROW

Illustrated by

EMMA CHICHESTER CLARK

Kingfisher

KINGFISHER

An imprint of Larousse plc
Elsley House, 24–30 Great Titchfield Street
London W1P 7AD

First published by Kingfisher 1996
2 4 6 8 10 9 7 5 3 1

Educational Adviser: Prue Goodwin
Reading and Language Centre
University of Reading

A CIP catalogue record for this book
is available from the British Library

ISBN 0 7534 0017 0

Series Editor: Caroline Walsh
Printed in Singapore

Contents

Chapter One

This is Miss Wire.

She was old

but she was full of life.

She had a little bird.

He was full of life, too.

4

Miss Wire was rather short
but her full name was very very long.
Her full name was
Miss Julia Johnson
Dickson Thompson
Annie Maria Wire.

Miss Wire lived with her friends at
The Hideaway Home
at Over-the-Hill,
near Faraway.

Most of Miss Wire's friends
were sleepy all the time.

They slept in their beds,

in their armchairs,

at the table,

and in front of the TV.

But not Miss Wire....

Miss Wire liked

to stay wide awake.

She wanted to have fun.

"Tonight is Christmas Eve!" she called.

"Wake up! Put out your stockings!"

"Oh ha-ha, Julia," said the old people.

"Very funny!

Christmas is not for old people.

Christmas is just for children!"

"Quite right!" said Matron.
"Santa is far too busy
to worry about old people at Christmas!"
Matron looked very wise
in her clean white collar
and her clean white cuffs
and her ever so

                    ever so

stiff white apron.
And she clapped
her clean white hands.
"Bedtime everyone!"
she said.

"That means you, Miss Wire."

Clap clap clap.

But Miss Wire didn't go to bed.

The Hideaway Home,
Over the Hill,
Faraway.

Christmas Eve
at 10 o' clock.

Dear Santa,
Sorry to bother you;
My friends are very, very old.
They think that
CHRISTMAS IS NOT FOR
OLD PEOPLE.

Can you help?
I hope I am not too late.
I am sending this by small
bird.
Love from
Julia Johnson Dickson
Thompson Annie Maria
Wire (aged 95)

Miss Wire wrote a letter.

And this is the letter

that Miss Wire wrote.

12

The little bird
took the letter in his beak
and flew as fast as he could
to the North Pole. Meanwhile....

13

Chapter Two

These are three little Christmas Mice.

They came sailing in

on three ships

on Christmas Day in the morning.

The three Christmas Mice

were full of life.

They called for their friends

at many a mousehole.

Most little mice

were having a long Winter sleep.

They slept in their nests

in their larders

and all squeezed up together.

But not the Christmas Mice....

15

They liked
to stay wide awake.
They wanted to have fun.
They threw snowballs,
and that was good fun.

They slid on the ice,
and that was good fun.
They made a snowmouse,
and that was good fun.

"But it's Christmas Morning!" they said.
"It would be much more fun
to help Father Christmas!
And they ran to find
a telephone.

Chapter Three

When the telephone rang,
Santa was sitting on his bed,
wearing his scarlet pyjamas,
reading Miss Wire's letter.

"Hello," said Santa.

"Hello, Santa. Do you want any help?" asked the Christmas Mice.

"How kind! Help is just what I need," said Santa.

"A little bird came to me this Christmas Morning with a letter.

It is from Miss Julia Johnson Dickson Thompson Annie Maria Wire (aged 95).

She sounds very sad.

She says that her old friends did not put out their stockings.

They think Christmas is just for children."

"Are there any presents left?"
asked the Christmas Mice.
"There are some bright balloons
and nothing else," said Santa. "Except..."
"Except what?" said the Christmas Mice.
"Except the Unwanted Toys," said Santa.

"The Unwanted Toys?

Why are they unwanted?"

asked the Christmas Mice.

"People say they are dangerous,"

said Santa. "They hide in the Dark Places

afraid that they will harm the children."

"We know the Dark Places,"
said the Christmas Mice.
"We shall find these Unwanted Toys
and show the old people
that Christmas is not just for children."
"My reindeer are tired," said Santa.
"Too tired to deliver the Unwanted Toys.
So who will deliver them?"

"Don't worry.

Just ask Miss Wire's little bird

to bring us the balloons,"

said the Christmas Mice.

"And hurry!"

Chapter Four

This is the wardrobe

in a Dark Dark Place.

The dust lay on the top as thick as tar.

Under the dust there was a cardboard box.

And in the box, a model racing car.

It had sharp bits sticking out all over.

The mice tapped twice upon the dusty box.

The car said,

"Leave me in this dark dark room!"

"Somebody wants you,"

said the Christmas Mice.

"So hurry, racer,

you were born to brrrrrrm!"

The little bird tied
a big yellow balloon
to the car and it flew
out of the window.

This is the shed where no one ever went.

High on a shelf and hidden at the back,

behind some tins and jars

there was a chest.

And in the chest,

a tin duck that went quack.

He had little flat feet

that went up and down.

"Come on!" the mice said,

lifting up the lid.

"Somebody needs you.

We must go to him."

"No!" sobbed the duck.

"What if I should rust?"

"Don't cry," the mice said.

"You were born to swim!"

The little bird tied on
a big red balloon
and the duck
flew out of the window.

This is the toyshop
where they kept the trunk.

Look what it said:

"A Merry Christmas!"

said the Christmas Mice.

"You are all wanted.

Will you come with us?"

And one by one

out crept the DANGEROUS toys.

31

The cuddly toys said:

"What if the babies swallow our eyes!"

The clockwork trains said:

"What if our wheels come off?"

The tin planes said:

"Small children will cut their hands on us!"

The lead soldiers said:

"Little boys will put us in their mouths!"

The glass marbles and the china dolls

were afraid they might shatter.

"Look out, look out when we're about!"
said the spud-guns.

"Look out for your eyes!"
cried the bows and arrows, the swords,
the penknives and the catapults.

"Look out for your fingers!"
said the carpentry sets

and the building sets and chemistry sets.

"Don't worry!" said the Christmas Mice.
"We know a place where every toy here
will bring nothing but happiness."

And soon all the Unwanted Toys were flying over the hills to Faraway. The little bird and the Christmas Mice followed close behind.

Chapter Five

On Christmas Morning

at the Hideaway Home

– Suddenly! –

all the beds were full of cuddly toys.

All the baths were full
of clockwork ducks and tugs
and swimming frogs!

All the carpets were covered
with racing cars and tin trains!

And saws were sawing at table legs

and spud guns went pop

and arrows flew

and sword-fighters went

one-two, one-two

and dollies were dressed

and then undressed

and growly teddies

got their tummies pressed

and marbles got flicked

and went ting and tang

and chemistry sets went

WHIFF! and BANG!!!

And all the old people said,
"These toys are *just*
what we always wanted!
Who can we thank
for our best Christmas *ever*?"
"Well," said Miss Wire,
"my little bird tells me
that you must thank
the Christmas Mice."
"Three cheers and thanks
to the Christmas Mice!"
cried the old people.
"And three cheers and thanks
to our Miss Wire,"
cried Matron.

"For she has taught me

that Christmas is not just for children.

Christmas is for *everyone*."

And Matron pulled off

her clean white collar

and her clean white cuffs

and her ever so

          ever so

stiff white apron.

"Come on, everyone," she cried.

"Let's play pirates!"

And everyone joined in.

The little bird joined in.

So did the Christmas Mice,

and the old people.

And so did Miss Julia Johnson

Dickson Thompson

Annie Maria Wire (aged 95).

They all had a rollocking jollocking
rough tough time.
And as for the Unwanted Toys,
they were never unwanted again.

 THE END

About the Author and Illustrator

Ian Whybrow is the author of the *The Shrinky Kid Stories* and of *Quacky Quack Quack*, which was shortlisted for the Smarties Award. He says, "I really like the idea of old people playing with toys that are too dangerous for small children. We all need toys no matter what age we are!"

Emma Chichester Clark won the Mother Goose Award with her first book and is now one of the most popular children's book illustrators. "I enjoyed drawing Miss Wire," says Emma. "She has a lot of spirit – I hope I'm like her when I'm 95."

If you've enjoyed reading
Miss Wire and the Three Kind Mice,
try these other **I Am Reading** books:

ALLIGATOR TAILS AND CROCODILE CAKES
Nicola Moon & Andy Ellis

KIT'S CASTLE
Chris Powling & Anthony Lewis

MR COOL
Jacqueline Wilson & Stephen Lewis

WATCH OUT, WILLIAM
Kady MacDonald Denton

BARN PARTY
Claire O'Brien & Tim Archbold